TANTRUM TABITHA
by TONY GARTH

Tabitha didn't need a reason to throw a tantrum.

It didn't matter where she was, who she was with or what she was doing..., she could always throw a tantrum.

Sometimes her tantrums were so terrible that she rolled around the floor, kicked her legs in the air and screamed until she went blue in the face!

One day, Tabitha went shopping with her Mum.

At the greengrocer's, her Mum bought some sprouts. And Tabitha had a tantrum.

She screamed and shrieked. "I hate sprouts! I hate sprouts!" she screeched. "They're horrible!"

So, her Mum put the sprouts back and picked up some carrots instead. But it just made Tabitha worse. She hated carrots too, and broccoli, and cabbage!

As they waited for the bus to go home, Tabitha threw another tantrum.

"I hate the bus! I hate it! I hate it!" she yelled. And she clung to the bus stop and screamed.

Tabitha's Mum called for a taxi. But Tabitha hated taxis too. She started to scream even louder!

When they got home at last, Tabitha had a tantrum over dinner.

And when it was bathtime, she had another tantrum. She hated baths. She hated soap. She hated having her hair washed. And she hated having to clean her teeth.

Then she had a tantrum about going to bed.

Next day, she went with her Mum to visit her Grandma.

Tabitha didn't want to go. As soon as they got to Grandma's house, Tabitha threw a tantrum. She screamed and rolled around on the carpet while her Mum and Grandma had a chat and tried to ignore her.

"I just don't know what to do with her," said Tabitha's Mum.

"Don't worry," said Grandma. "I've got an idea."

And she leaned over to whisper her plan.

On the way home, they passed the greengrocer's shop again.

"I'm not buying any vegetables today, Tabitha," her Mum said. "Because I know how much you hate them."

Tabitha's face began to twist - she was about to throw a terrible tantrum.

"What will we have for dinner then?" she asked.

"Nothing," her Mum replied. "There's no dinner today. Because I know how much you hate it."

The bus went straight by. Tabitha's screwed her face up some more.

"We've missed the bus," she wailed.

"We're not catching the bus today," said her Mum. "You hate the bus so we're going to walk."

It was a very long walk home. Soon Tabitha had a tantrum.

"I hate walking," she screamed. "And my feet hurt. Why can't we get the bus?"

"We can go by bus any time you like," replied her Mum. "On one condition. That you promise not to have a tantrum."

Tabitha promised. Her feet hurt too much to argue.

At dinner time, the table was bare. And Tabitha had another tantrum.

"I want my dinner!" she shrieked. "I'm hungry."

"I'll make you some dinner," said her Mum. "If you promise there'll be no more tantrums at dinner time."

It was a difficult decision, but Tabitha promised. Her tummy was rumbling quite badly by now.

Bathtime came round and Tabitha started to work herself up into a tantrum.

"I'm sorry, Tabitha," said her Mum. "But you can't have a bath tonight."

Tabitha wailed and yelled.

"BUT I WANT ONE," she screamed. "It's not fair!"

"Well, I'm sorry," said her Mum. "But you just can't have one."

Tabitha screamed even louder.

"Very well," said her Mum. "You can have a bath if you promise to stop this tantrum."

"All right," agreed Tabitha. "But only if I can have soap, shampoo and everything."

Her Mum nodded and Tabitha promised. That night she had her first tantrum-free bath!

Tabitha got ready for bed.

"Bedtime's banned!" her Mum announced.
"You'll have to stay up forever!"

Tabitha thought hard. She decided not to throw a tantrum this time. She quite liked the idea of staying up forever. That evening she watched TV until her eyes went square...

"Please can I go to bed now, Mum," she asked, politely. "I'm really tired and I can't keep my eyes open."

Her Mum looked very surprised!

"Please, Mum," said Tabitha again. "If you don't let me, I'll scream!"

Collect all 30 titles in the Little Monsters series